# MICH...

# Pad...

## AND AUNT LUCY

### Illustrated by Barry Wilkinson

COLLINS COLOUR CUBS

Paddington's Aunt Lucy was staying with the Brown family, and there was great excitement the first morning when Mrs. Bird brought the breakfast tray down from her room.

"Well," she said, "I can see where Paddington gets his appetite from and no mistake. Aunt Lucy polished that off in no time at all. Now she wants to go out."

The words were hardly out of Mrs. Bird's mouth when Aunt Lucy herself appeared, dressed in all her finery.

"*I'm* ready," she said pointedly.

"Oh, dear," said Mrs. Brown, nervously. "We haven't really had time to plan anything yet."

"How about going to the Tower of London?" suggested Judy.

"Or Buckingham Palace?" broke in Jonathan.

Aunt Lucy held up her paw. "I'd like to go to Barkridges if I may. Paddington's told me all about it." She looked round carefully in order to make sure Mr. Brown was nowhere in sight. "I want to buy a certain person a Christmas present.

"It's been a great comfort to me over the years to know that Paddington's been looked after and it would be nice to do something in return."

"It's very kind of you," said Mrs. Brown. She thought for a moment. "How about some pipe-cleaners?"

"*Pipe cleaners!*" exclaimed Aunt Lucy. "I want something more than that. Besides, it ought to be something you can all enjoy."

"How about something for an inflatable dinghy?" suggested Paddington, as he came into the hall and overheard what was going on. "Mr. Brown's been talking about buying one for a long time now."

"That," said Aunt Lucy approvingly, "sounds a *much* better idea."

If the man in charge of the boat depart-
ment at Barkridges was surprised by the
sudden crowd of customers, he did his best
to conceal it.

"What can I do for you?" he asked, rubbing his hands in anticipation.

"This lady would like something small for an inflatable dinghy," said Mrs. Brown.

The man's face fell. "How about a pump?" he suggested. "Or a puncture outfit?"

Paddington gave him a hard stare. "A *puncture outfit?*" he repeated indignantly. "Mr. Brown hasn't even got his boat yet!"

Having put the assistant in his place, Paddington gazed round the shop and saw to his surprise that Aunt Lucy was trying to clamber into a large rubber dinghy which occupied a position of honour in the middle of the show-room.

"This looks very interesting," she said.

The salesman's face lit up as he rushed forward to help.

"I can see I'm dealing with a lady of taste," he exclaimed, picking up a small canvas bag. "That happens to be our very best self-inflating model dinghy. It blows itself up in a matter of seconds. All you do is pull this cord and stand well clear.

"As you can see, it comes complete with automatic radio, distress flares, sea-sickness pills. There's even a packet of emergency boiled sweets . . ."

"I know," said Aunt Lucy happily. "I've found them. Bears like boiled sweets." She felt in her purse. "I'll take one."

"But you can't buy the *whole* boat!" cried Mrs. Brown. "It's much too expensive."

Aunt Lucy helped herself to some more boiled sweets. "I have my savings," she said, "crunch ... crunch ... *and* Paddington's allowance ... crunch ... crunch."

Paddington hurried forward to help Aunt Lucy out of the dinghy.

"I always put some by out of my bun money," he explained.

"I've got lots of postal orders," agreed Aunt Lucy, "but I've never . . . crunch . . . cashed them until now . . . crunch . . . crunch. I've been saving them for a special occasion."

The Browns gazed at each other. It was the first they had ever heard of Paddington making his Aunt Lucy an allowance.

"The ways of bears are dark and mysterious," began Mrs. Bird, voicing the thoughts of them all. Then she broke off as a loud moan came from somewhere close at hand.

"Ooooooooh!" groaned Aunt Lucy. "Ooooooooooh! I feel sick!"

"I bet it's all those boiled sweets," murmured Judy. "She must have eaten most of the packet."

"Hold on!" cried Paddington, rushing to
the rescue. "I'll get you a sea-sickness pill."

"Watch out!" yelled the shop assistant, as Paddington made a dive for the canvas bag.

'Oooooh!" moaned Aunt Lucy, louder than ever. "Hurry!"

"Don't worry!" exclaimed Paddington.
"I can feel them. They're tied up . . . Oh!"

Paddington nearly fell over backwards
with alarm as a hiss of escaping air came
from somewhere inside the bag.

"Oh, dear!" he exclaimed. "I think I may
have pulled the wrong string by mistake."

Any thoughts Paddington might have had about stopping the boat from inflating disappeared as it slowly but surely billowed forth.

"Help!" cried Aunt Lucy, as she rose higher and higher into the air.

"Oh, my word!" gasped the assistant, as she fell over backwards and disappeared from view in a whirl of masts, radio signals, flares and flashing lights.

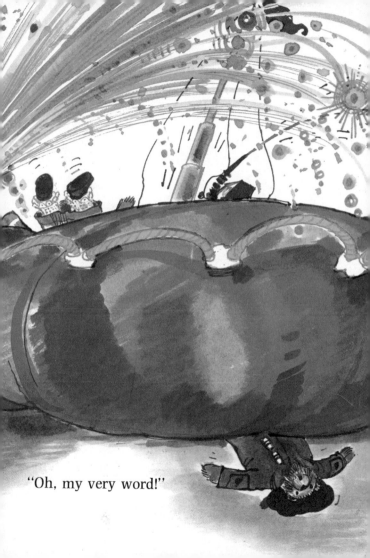

"Oh, my very word!"

He turned to the Browns. "Will Modom be taking it with her?" he enquired stiffly.

"I think," said Mrs. Bird, "in the circumstances, we'd best be taking Modom with us."

Aunt Lucy retired to bed early that night, but before she went upstairs she solemnly shook hands with everyone and gave them each a present.

Mr. Brown could hardly believe his eyes when he saw his, and there was a Peruvian shawl for Mrs. Brown and Mrs. Bird, a dressing gown for Paddington . . .

. . . not to mention a large jar of honey each for Jonathan and Judy.

"Made," said Aunt Lucy, "by the bees who live in the Home for Retired Bears in Lima. It's very sweet because they're always getting at the marmalade."

"How very thoughtful," said Mrs. Brown, as the door closed behind Paddington and Aunt Lucy.

Then she broke off and looked at Mrs. Bird. "Is anything the matter?" she asked. "You looked worried."

"You don't think," said Mrs. Bird, "that she's planning on taking Paddington back to Peru with her, do you?"

A sudden chill came over everyone.

"It's really up to them to decide," she continued. "We can't stop him if he wants to go."

The Browns slept very badly that night.
The thought of life without Paddington was
hard to take in, and they breathed a sigh of
relief when they came downstairs next
morning and found him already sitting at
the breakfast table.

Mrs. Brown glanced round the room.
"Where's Aunt Lucy?" she asked.
"She's gone," said Paddington sadly.
"Gone!" echoed the Browns.

"Aunt Lucy doesn't like goodbyes," explained Paddington. "Besides, she was only on an excursion."

"But she left this note for you."

"Thank you very much for having me and for looking after Paddington so well," read Jonathan.

"Now that I've got used to it," continued Judy, "it does seem a funny name for a railway station. Happy sailing! Aunt Lucy."

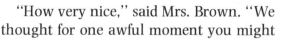

"How very nice," said Mrs. Brown. "We thought for one awful moment you might be going back with her."

Paddington nearly fell off his seat with surprise at the thought. "*Go back to Peru!*" he exclaimed. "I'm not old enough to *retire*! Besides, I don't think Aunt Lucy would like to think of me doing that . . . even if I wanted to . . . which I don't . . .

. . . I'm much too happy where I am."

*This story comes from*
*"Comings and Goings at Number 32" in*
PADDINGTON ON TOP
*and is based on the television film.*
*It has been specially written by*
*Michael Bond for younger children.*

ISBN 0 00 123541 9
Text copyright © 1980 Michael Bond
Illustrations copyright © 1980 William Collins Sons & Co Ltd.
Cover copyright © 1980 William Collins Sons & Co Ltd.
and Film Fair Ltd./Paddington & Co Ltd.
Cover design by Linda Sullivan.
Cover photographed by Barry Macey
Printed in Great Britain